Let's Be Safe

Let's Be Safe

P. K. Hallinan

ideals children's books.

Nashville, Tennessee

ISBN-13: 978-0-8249-5529-8

Published by Ideals Children's Books
An imprint of Ideals Publications
A Guideposts Company
Nashville, Tennessee
www.idealsbooks.com

Color separations by Precision Color Graphics, Franklin, Wisconsin
Printed and bound in the United States of America

Library of Congress Cataloging-in-Publication Data

Hallinan, P. K.
  Let's be safe / by P.K. Hallinan.
      p. cm.
  Summary: Simple, rhyming text presents situations in which a child
must take precautions in order to stay safe throughout the day, both at
home and at play.
  ISBN 978-0-8249-5529-8 (alk. paper)
  [1. Safety--Fiction. 2. Stories in rhyme.] I. Title. II. Title: Let us be
safe.
  PZ8.3.H15Lcj 2007
  [E]--dc22
                              2007007734

Designed by Georgina Chidlow-Rucker

10 9 8 7 6 5 4 3 2

This book is for

_____

◆   ◆   ◆

From

_____

I like to be careful,
So I try to obey

The best tips for safety
As I go through my day.

I'm patient at crosswalks—
I wait to be crossed.

I follow directions
So I won't become lost.

I keep on the lookout
For pitfalls and snares.

I avoid taking chances
Or ridiculous dares.

I even act safely
When lifting some weight.
I bend at the knees,
But I keep my back straight!

Yes, safety requires a more thoughtful way
Of doing those things I enjoy every day.
So I put on my helmet when riding my bike.

I wear sturdy shoes
When I go for a hike.

When on my skateboard,
All you can see

Are scads of safe pads
From my head to my knees!

I wear cotton gloves
For splinters or thorns.

I stay close to home
If it looks like a storm.

I like to be cautious
And let sleeping dogs lie.

And I don't talk with strangers—
I just travel on by.

Yes, safety's important
In so many ways.
I wear lots of sunscreen
On bright sunny days.

And I never go swimming
At a pool or the beach
If someone's not with me
And well within reach!

I watch where I'm going
When I'm running or skipping.

I tie my shoelaces
To avoid any tripping.

When playing sports
The idea's the same—

I wear the protection
That comes with the game!

Even when I'm camping,
I'm happy to stay

Real close to the campground
And not wander away.

Yes, I try to be careful—
It's the least I can be
For all of those people . . .

Who care about me.